Tee and Mo

Only One Mum

© 2023 Plug-In Productions Limited & Tee and Mo Productions Limited

Only One Mum is based on the original song written in 2018 by Dominic Minns, Joss Peach and Ellie Wyatt.

Only One Mum was first published in the United Kingdom by HarperCollins *Children's Books* in 2023 and was adapted from the original song by Rebecca Gerlings.

HarperCollins *Children's Books* is a division of HarperCollins*Publishers* Ltd,
1 London Bridge Street, London SE1 9GF

www.harpercollins.co.uk

HarperCollins*Publishers*
Macken House, 39/40 Mayor Street Upper
Dublin 1, DO1 C9W8, Ireland

10 9 8 7 6 5 4 3 2 1

ISBN: 978-0-00-854284-9

Printed in Great Britain by Bell and Bain Ltd, Glasgow

MIX
Paper | Supporting
responsible forestry
FSC™ C007454

This book is produced from independently certified FSC™ paper
to ensure responsible forest management.

For more information visit: www.harpercollins.co.uk/green

This is a story about **Tee** and **Mo**,
a **little monkey** and his
monkey mum who sometimes
want to do **different things** . . .
but **always** end up having
fun together.

It's Mother's Day.

Tee's friends are helping him think of ways to show Mo how MUCH he **loves** her.

VRRRM!

RAAH!

"I gave my mum a card," says Tomo.

"What about flowers?" suggests Lily.

"I made my mum breakfast!" says Nina.

"I want to give Mo something **extra** special . . ." replies Tee.

"GOT IT!" he shouts. He starts to rummage in his cupboards and drawers.

"Come on, everyone. I need your help!"

Mo can hear the rumpus from the kitchen.
RUMBLE! BASH! CRASH!

"Sandwiches are ready!" she calls over the noise. "Come and get 'em!"

But no one comes.

"**Tee?**" Mo calls again.

Still no answer – but a lot of giggling and the sound of footsteps rushing past!

HA HA HA!
HEE HEE HEE!

She peeps inside the living room . . .

and sees Tee standing on a home-made stage.

TA-DAH!

Mo's so surprised she nearly drops the sandwiches!

Tee clears his throat . . . **"Ahem."**

"**Nobody** else could do what you do. You're the mum with the fun, you make sandwiches yum and you're really good at stories **too!**"

"Mum, Mum, Mum, Mum, Mum, Mum, Mummy, oh, Mummy, oh, Ma!"

sing his friends.

Mo beams.

Tee drags Mo towards the front door while continuing his song.

"**Mama**, where's my shoe? There's no one else here
to ask, **only you!** I want to take you **out on the town.**
But first, can we hit the playground?"

Tomo, Lily and Nina whizz down the slide singing,
"Mum, Mum, Mum, Mum, Mum, Mum,
Mummy, oh, Mummy, oh, Ma!"

WEEEEE!

Mo chuckles. How did
they get there?

Tee and his friends take turns on the slide.

WEEEEEE!

WA-HOO!

Tee breaks into song as he somersaults off the end:

"There are millions of mums, but I've only got **onnnnne!**"

"And if I had to choose," he adds, "I would **probably** choose **you.**"

"Probably?" teases Mo.

"DEFINITELY!" Tee corrects himself, giving her a **smacker** of a kiss.

MWAH!

It's time for Tomo,
Lily and Nina to head back
to their own mamas.

"That was fun,
Tee – see you later!"
they call.

Tee waves.
"Thanks for
helping!"
he says.

"Nice teamwork!"
says Mo, impressed.

"Thanks!" replies Tee.
"I learned from
the best."

"Remember when we pretended to be sea monsters?" says Mo, chuckling.

Splash! Splosh!

RAHHHHHHHHHHHHHHHH!

"And when we made up that song together?" replies Tee.

Tinkle-tinkle-tinkle!

BANG! BANG! BANG! BANG!

"**Ooh-ooh!** Remember when we lost that piece of our favourite jigsaw?"

Snip!
Snip!
Snip!

Ah-ah-ah!

Hee!
Hee!
Hee!

"And **don't forget** our SUPERHERO CAR WASH!" adds Tee.

OO-AH-OOOOOOOOO!

Action Ape and Monkey Mum **saved the day!**

"Not bad, are we?" agrees Mo. "No matter what comes our way, I'll **always** be your mummy—"

Tee stomps through a muddy puddle.

Splat!

Splat! . . .

"And I'll always be your little monkey!" says Tee, jumping into Mo's arms.

. . . Splat!

"That's better. Who needs to hit the town when you can have a nice bath instead," says Mo with a chuckle.

"Out of all the millions of mums, I would certainly, definitely, totally, ABSOLUTELY choose you," says Tee, as Mo dries him off.

"Always?"
asks Mo.

"Always!"
declares Tee.

Mo snuggles
Tee tight in his
bath towel.

There's just **one last thing** Tee needs
to say — and it has to be back on stage.

"And I hope you'd choose me toooo!"

he sings.

Mo's heart is ready to burst.

"Ahhh, **of course**," she gasps.

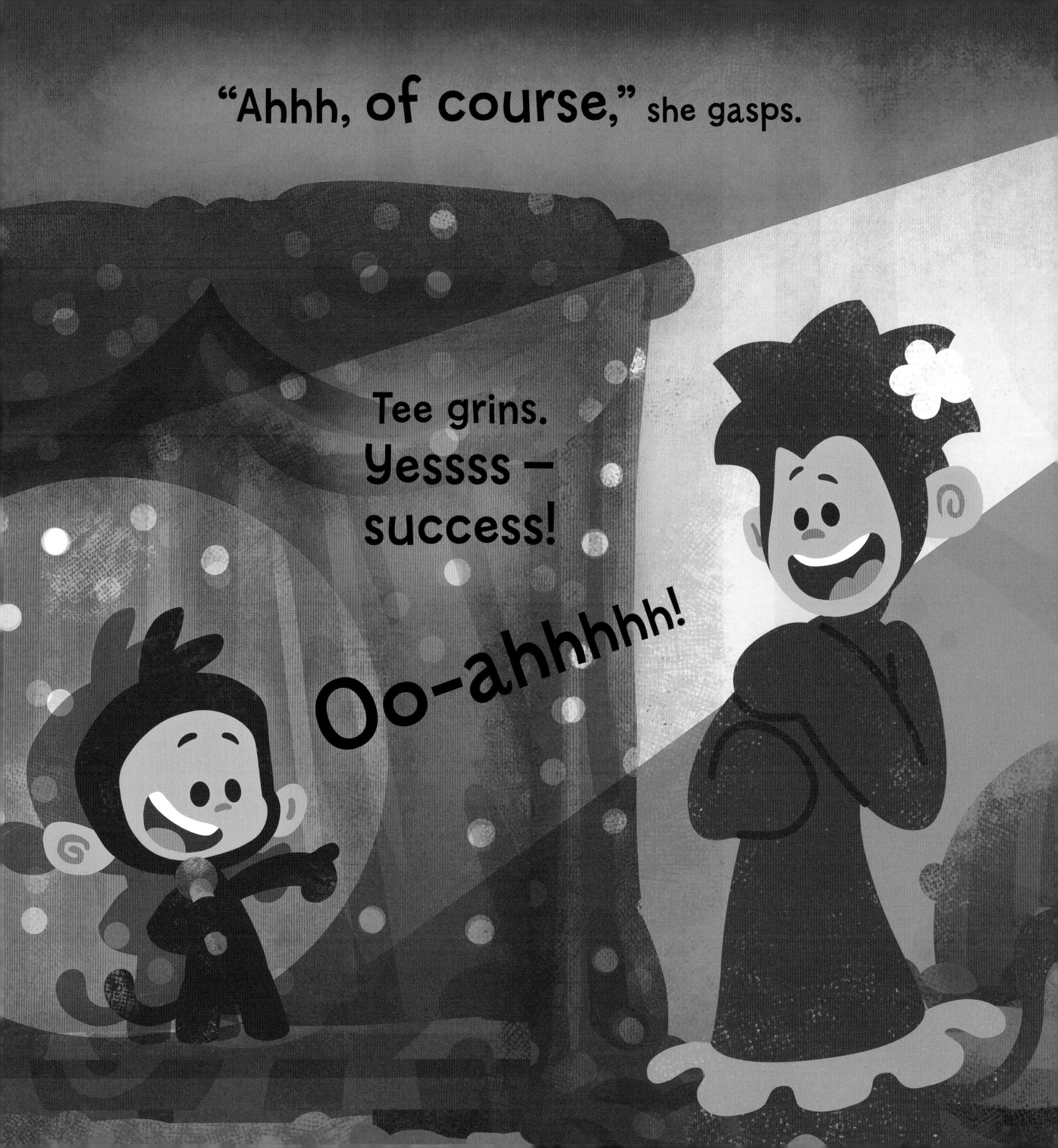

Tee grins.
Yessss – success!

Oo-ahhhhh!

"Happy Mother's Day, Mo," says Tee, giving her another snuggle.

"Thank you, Tee," replies Mo. "It's been **extra special.**"

"All that singing has made me **hungry,**" says Tee.

"Let's have those sandwiches," says Mo.

"**Yum!**" replies Tee.
OO-AH!

Only One Mum

Oh, Mama, I love you!
Nobody else could do what you do.
You're the mum with the fun,
You make sandwiches yum,
And you're really good at stories too!
Oh, Mama, where's my shoe?
There's no one else here to ask, only you!
Wanna take you out on the town,
But first can we hit the playground?

CHORUS
There are millions of mums,
But I've only got one!
If I had to choose,
I would probably,
Definitely,
Choose you!
Oh, Mama, you're a dream!
'Cause me and you are the best-ever team!
No matter what comes our way,
You'll be my mummy and I'll be your baby!

Turn the page to play the song using our special QR code!

There are millions of mums,
But I've only got one!
If I had to choose,
I would certainly,
Definitely,
Totally,
Absolutely,
Choose you!
I'm talking to you, Mama, out of everyone
  in the world, I would always choose you,
And I'd hope you choose me too!

Scan the QR code
with your phone to hear
the original song sung by
Lauren Laverne

www.harpercollinschildrensbooks.co.uk/teeandmo